You are Molly. You and Thistle, the little halfling, follow the Good Knight of the Golden Dragon and his soldiers to SHADOWCASTLE in search of your friend and Thistle's brother.

You might be a kid, but you're brave! And you can outsmart any creatures you meet on the way . . . you hope!

A giant ogre's footsteps shake the ground as it stomps toward the castle guardhouse where you're hiding.

Will you run for the woods to escape?

Or will you pull the glowing stone from your pocket, say the magic words, and hope it gets you out of this mess?

The choice is yours!

Shadowcastle

by Michael Gray

Illustrated by Mario Macari, Jr.
Cover art by Clyde Caldwell

TSR, Inc.

For Molly Marissa —
the sunshine of my life.

Distributed to the book trade in the United States by Random House, Inc. and in Canada by Random House of Canada, Ltd.
Distributed in the United Kingdom by TSR (UK), Ltd.
Distributed to the toy and hobby trade by regional distributors.

DUNGEONS & DRAGONS, D&D, FANTASY FOREST, and PICK A PATH TO ADVENTURE are trademarks owned by TSR, Inc.

First Printing: October, 1983
Printed in the United States of America.
Library of Congress Catalog Card Number: 83-50983
ISBN: 0-88038-061-6

9 8 7 6 5 4 3 2 1

TSR, Inc.
P.O. Box 756
Lake Geneva, WI 53147

TSR (UK), Ltd.
The Mill, Rathmore Road
Cambridge CB1 4AD
United Kingdom

Stop!

Don't turn this page yet!

You're about to set out on not one, but many great adventures! Here's all you have to do—

To start your adventure, turn to page seven and begin. Read until you come to a set of choices. Pick one and follow the directions.

As you read, keep making choices and following the directions until the story ends. Then start at the beginning again and pick other choices. Each one will take you on a different adventure.

All right, go ahead and turn the page . . .

You are picking moonberries when you hear something moving through the grass farther down the hill.

Peering over the bushes, you see a strange little man push his way through the high green grass. He's only three feet tall and barefoot. His head bobs up and down as he hurries along the path.

"Hey, little man! Where are you going?" you shout to him. Startled, he jumps off the pathway. A few seconds later, you see his little face watching you from under a leafy plant to the side of the path.

"Are you alone?" he asks.

"Oh, yes," you tell him. "Please come up here and tell me about yourself."

He climbs slowly up the hill toward you and says, "Before I tell you who I am, who are you?"

"My name is Molly," you tell him, "and I live on a farm near this berry patch. I was picking a basketful of these moonberries when I saw you tramping through the grass. Who are you? And why are you such a little man?"

"I'm a halfling," he says. "You may call me Thistle. I am off to climb the Cragg and rescue my brother."

"The Cragg!" you say with fear as you look up at that jagged mountain peak. "Monsters live there. They come down at night and steal my father's cows.

"My friend Garth once told me that the monsters were created by an evil skeleton wizard called Nightshade. Garth has been missing since last night. Do you think the monsters captured him?"

"I wouldn't doubt it," Thistle says.

He lowers his voice and whispers, "When my brother disappeared two nights ago, I found strange footprints outside our cottage. I figured he'd been taken prisoner. I hope I find him.

"Would you like to come with me?" he asks. "We might find your friend, too."

If you would like to go, turn to page 10.

If you decide to stay out of danger and pick berries, turn to page 15.

"I'd like to go on an adventure," you say. You pick up your basket and set off after the halfling. Soon you hear the drumming of horses' hooves on the road at the bottom of the hill.

"Look!" says Thistle. "It's Sir Gregor, Good Knight of the Golden Dragon, and his soldiers. They're heading up the road to the Cragg. Let's go and talk to them!"

You both run down the grassy hillside to meet the brave warriors. The Good Knight sees you. He motions his troops to continue on up the road and guides his horse over to you and Thistle.

"Greetings, brave one!" says Thistle. He bows to the famous knight. "What evil are you fighting now?"

"I'm off to Shadowcastle on the Cragg to fight Nightshade," the Good Knight says. "My men and I are going to put an end to the stealing and kidnapping that have been going on around here."

"Good luck to you, sir!" you say.

"Thank you, friend," the Good Knight says, and rides off to join his men.

"Let's follow them," the halfling says.
"They'll fight all the monsters. When we
get to Nightshade's castle, we'll look for my
brother and your friend."

"All right," you agree. "Let's go."

After you follow the road for a while,
Thistle points out a path on the right.

"Maybe it's a shortcut to the castle," you
say. "Let's take a look."

You turn off the road and onto the path.
You push past some low branches and find
yourselves at the edge of a small pond

ringed by trees. Thistle grabs your arm and whispers, "Shhhh! Look over there."

Looking across the pond, you see two strange creatures. They look like men with frogs' heads! They're holding wooden spears and croaking at each other.

If you want to meet the strange creatures, turn to page 19.

If you want to return to the road, turn to page 23.

"No, that sounds too dangerous to me," you tell him. "I'd rather pick berries."

He looks at you sadly, says good-bye, and hurries back down to the path. Then you hear the sound of horses. Sir Gregor, Good Knight of the Golden Dragon, and his soldiers are riding up the road to the Cragg.

Thistle runs to greet them, but he trips and rolls down the hill in a cloud of dust! You pick up your basket and run down to see if he's all right.

By the time you reach him, he is sitting up and brushing the dust off his clothes.

"I thought you wanted to pick berries," he says in a huff.

"Well, I changed my mind," you tell him, deciding that you might be able to help.

When you look up, you see that most of the soldiers have passed. The last soldier turns his horse toward you.

"Hello, little ones," he says. "You'd better head home. There'll be a lot of fighting going on soon up at Shadowcastle."

"What is Shadowcastle?" you ask.

"It's Nightshade's castle on the Cragg, where the monsters live!"

You notice the soldier's beautiful warhorse as it snatches a berry from your basket. "That's a wonderful horse you have," you tell him.

"Thank you," he says as he hands you three lumps of sugar from his saddlebag. "But he should know better than to eat moonberries," he tells you. "They put most animals to sleep, you know."

You hold one lump in your open hand. The horse nibbles the sugar from your palm and then rubs his nose against your cheek.

It tickles and makes you laugh.

The soldier says, "I have to catch up with the rest of the men! Good-bye!" He waves at you and rides off. You put the other lumps of sugar into your pocket.

"Let's follow the soldiers," Thistle says. "While they fight the monsters, we'll search for my brother and your friend Garth."

"That makes sense," you say. "Let's go."

After walking for a mile, you come upon a cave opening in the side of the mountain.

"Maybe my brother's being held prisoner in that cave," Thistle says as you walk over to the entrance. "Should we find out?"

"Let's go back to the road and keep following the soldiers," you say. Turn to page 23.

"All right. Let's go inside," you say. Turn to page 25.

"Let's go and talk to them, Thistle. Maybe they'll know if this is a shortcut," you say as you walk out of the bushes.

"Oh, no, Molly!" cries Thistle. "Those creatures are bullywugs. They're mean and fierce—and they've got spears. Come on! Let's run before they see us."

But it's too late. The froglike creatures have seen you walk out of the woods. They start hopping toward you!

You and Thistle turn and dodge into the trees to your right. The jumping bullywugs are close behind you, waving their spears.

Running through a field of ferns, you hear the bullywugs croaking nearby. They're gaining on you!

Thinking fast, you see a tree ahead and get an idea. "Let's climb that big tree," you say, pointing to a tall chestnut tree.

"Sounds like a good idea to me," Thistle replies, breathing hard.

Thistle reaches the tree first and scrambles up to the first limb. You follow him with the basket of moonberries slung over your shoulder.

When the bullywugs reach the tree, they look up and see you sitting high above. One of them throws its spear at you! BONK! The spear hits a tree limb and falls back down. The bullywug starts to climb the tree!

You clutch your basket tighter, trying to think. Suddenly, you remember something your father told you about moonberries—when eaten, they put most animals to sleep!

"What now?" Thistle moans.

"We can use the basket of moonberries," you say. "I hope the bullywugs are hungry."

Now you have a choice. You could drop handfuls of berries and hope that the creatures will eat them and fall asleep.

Or you could drop the whole basket on one bullywug's head and knock it out.

If you want to drop a few handfuls of berries on the creatures to see what they'll do, turn to page 30.

If you want to drop the whole basket of berries on one creature's head, turn to page 37.

Returning to the road, you and Thistle follow it up the mountain. Soon the road levels off and you see before you a black, eerie-looking castle.

As you approach the castle, you take a deep breath, open the gate—and step into the midst of a battle between the Good Knight's warriors and the monsters!

Dodging fighters, you both race across the courtyard and through the main door to the castle itself. As you go through, two great golden doors ahead of you burst open.

There stands a huge monster with the body of a man and the head of a bull!

"A minotaur!" yells Thistle. "Run!"

Now that you're inside, you have only two ways to escape. You can either take stairs to a lower level, or go through an open door to a tower.

If you run down the stairway, turn to page 38.

If you run to the open door leading to a tower, turn to page 40.

As you enter the cave, you notice that your moonberries are beginning to glow. "So that's why everyone calls them MOONberries," you tell Thistle.

By the light of the berries, you creep into the dark cave. Looking down, you see a huge footprint in the dust. Deeper and deeper you go until you hear a gruff voice behind you say, "I'll get the halfling!"

Another voice says, "I'll get the girl!"

Turning around, you see a giant hand grab you. You scream as you are lifted high in the air. Your basket and berries go flying. Thistle shouts, "Let me down!"

Both of you are carried deeper into the cave. Without your berries, you can't see who or what is holding you. When your captor approaches a fire, you see that you have been caught by a two-headed giant!

"What shall we do with them?" one giant head asks the other.

"Lock them in the back room and eat them later," the other head says. Then you are thrown into a dark room at the end of the cave. A huge door slams shut!

As soon as your eyes get used to the dim
light that comes through cracks in the door,
you can see Thistle sitting on a rock with
his head in his hands. "This is it. We're
finished!" he moans.

"No, we're not!" you scold him. "Let's
find a way out of here!"

You go to the back of the room and begin
pulling rocks out of the wall. "Come on!
Help me, Thistle!" you plead.

After removing a few more rocks, you feel
a breeze blowing through a crack in the

wall. "There must be a way out behind this room. See if you can squeeze through."

Once through the wall, Thistle tells you to follow him. On your hands and knees, you crawl in the dark through the passageway. You bump your head. Ouch!

Then your hand touches a smooth stone, and it begins to give off a blue glow! A magic stone! You pick it up, and it lights your way out of the tunnel. When you near the end of the tunnel, you put the stone into your pocket.

At the end of the tunnel, you look up the mountain and see a black, eerie castle.

Then you hear a rattling sound coming from the rocks in front of you. The skull of a skeleton guard rises up above a boulder. You scream, "Thistle, look out!"

The skeleton climbs up over the boulder, reaching toward you. You pick up a rock and hurl it as hard as you can at the creature.

CRACK! The rock hits the skeleton and knocks its ugly skull off. You're saved!

You hear a shout and turn to see a

company of pig-faced soldiers running in
your direction! "Orcs!" you cry.

*If you want to run for the castle, turn to
page 45.*

*If you want to run back down the rocky
mountainside, turn to page 49.*

You drop a handful of berries at the bullywug in the tree. The berries bounce off its head and land on the ground. The other bullywug starts to eat them!

You drop another handful. The first creature opens its big mouth and catches the berries. It chews, then looks up and opens its mouth again. The other bullywug hops over and opens its mouth, too.

"This is fun!" you giggle. You hand a few berries to Thistle, and you both feed berries to the creatures.

After you've fed them about half your berries, you notice that they are starting to get sleepy. Soon they both sit down among the ferns and topple over!

Thistle chuckles. "Those berries of yours must have put the bullywugs to sleep! Let's get out of here before they wake up."

You both climb out of the tree, step over the sleeping bullywugs, and run off through the woods.

Back at the pond, you come upon a fallen log. "Why don't we stop and rest for a while?" you say.

You set your basket down and sit down on the mossy log. "I hope we find our way back to the road soon! Walking through all this brush is hard work!" you tell Thistle.

"It sure is!" he says. "But we must go on."

When you lean over to get your basket, a glint of metal inside the end of the hollow log catches your eye. Carefully, you reach in and pull out a dusty metal bowl.

"Hey, Thistle," you say, "look at this."

He takes the bowl from you and rubs it on the mossy log. "Molly, I think this bowl is made of silver!" he says as he shows you the area he cleaned off.

He hands it back, and you put it into your basket. Then you both get up and head around the pond. On the other side, you find the pathway back to the road.

Soon you climb out of the woods back onto the main road that leads up the mountainside. A few minutes later, you see the signs of a battle. Helmets, swords, and spears lie scattered on the road.

"That must be Shadowcastle ahead," Thistle says. Black and eerie, the evil fortress

juts out from the Cragg into dark, billowing clouds. A shiver runs down your back.

As you approach the evil castle, you can hear the clanging of weapons. Sneaking through the castle gate, you find yourselves in the middle of a battle between the Good Knight's soldiers and orc guards!

Dodging spears and swords, you head for the main door. Inside the castle, you see to your left a stairway leading down below the castle. Straight ahead are a pair of golden doors. To your right a door bursts open, and an orc guard runs straight at you!

If you want to run through the golden doors, turn to page 52.

If you want to run down the stairs, turn to page 54.

The creatures croak at each other and point up toward you.

The bullywug climbing the tree looks up. You drop the basket. BAM! It hits the creature's head, knocking the bullywug out of the tree!

Moonberries spill out all over the ground. To your relief, the bullywugs hop around and eat them as fast as they can.

Thistle laughs. "They like those berries as much as you do!"

One bullywug grabs the basket and munches down the rest of the berries. The other bullywug snatches the basket away. Finding it empty, the creature tears it in two and jumps on the other bullywug!

Then an amazing thing happens. One creature yawns. The other one yawns. Then both fall down and lie still.

"The berries worked!" you say. "They put the bullywugs to sleep!"

You climb down out of the tree and race back along the path to the road.

Please turn to page 23.

As you and Thistle run down the stairs to the dungeon, you can hear the minotaur bellowing behind you. "Hurry!" you shout.

Stepping through a doorway at the bottom of the stairs, you find yourselves in a great cavern. In the center of the cavern, some of the Good Knight's brave soldiers are fighting a nasty red dragon!

To your left, an underground waterfall flows out of a hole high in the wall.

The minotaur clumps down the stairs after you. "Quick! Hide behind the

waterfall!" you tell Thistle as you jump
behind the sheet of water.

When the minotaur enters the cavern, the
men and the dragon turn to attack it.

Suddenly, the dragon opens its mouth
and blows a jet of fire at the creature! The
minotaur bursts into flame and runs
howling out the door.

"Let's get out of here!" you cry. Then you
both run out the door and back up the
stairs. At the top of the stairs, you head for
the open tower door.

You go through the door and push your way past a broken chair. The room is empty except for a mop propped against a wall.

Thistle grabs the mop and says, "I'm going up to find my brother."

As he disappears up the stairs, you hear another voice shout, "Grix biggum!"

You then hear a scuffle, and Thistle shouts, "Take that, you nasty orc!"

A loud CLUNK echoes through the tower, and an orc guard comes tumbling down the stairs! You jump out of the way as the body rolls over to the corner and lies still.

The guard is knocked out but breathing. You notice a ring with three keys on it tied to the orc's belt. Grabbing the keys, you head up the stairs.

At the top of the stairs, you see another empty room. But this one has a barred door on one wall. Thistle, still holding the mop, stands on the first step of a stairway leading to the next floor.

"Ah! You've found the keys! Someone's in that cell. Let him out," says Thistle, pointing to the door.

You walk over and look into the cell.
Inside, looking back at you through the iron
bars, is your friend Garth! Hooray! You've
found him!

"Molly! Let me out of here!" he pleads.

"Garth, how did you get in there?" you
ask him as you unlock the cell door.

Garth tells you the whole story of how he
was kidnapped by a monster last night
behind the barn.

"I spent the whole night in this awful
place!" he tells you in a whisper.

Together you climb up the stairs to the next level.

In a room the same as the one below, you see Thistle talking to another halfling who is locked in another jail cell.

"Molly! It's my brother, Burr! We've found him!" he cries.

"Hello, Burr. This is my friend Garth. He was a prisoner downstairs," you tell the other halfling as you hurry to unlock his cell door.

"What happened to you?" Thistle asks his brother.

"I was gathering wood when something hit me on the head. I was knocked out," Burr says. "I woke up in this awful castle."

"Does Nightshade live here?" you ask.

"I think so," Burr replies. "The orcs say that the monsters and the castle were created by Nightshade's evil magic!"

You hear a sad moan come from above.

"Let's see who's upstairs and then get out of here!" Garth says to the group.

The four of you climb the stairs. At the top, you see another cell door, but no more stairs. This door is made of metal. You hear another moan come from behind the door.

Burr taps your shoulder. "I don't know what's in there, but let's leave it alone and get out of here."

If you want to leave the tower now, turn to page 58.

If you want to unlock the door, turn to page 60.

Staying low, you both run up toward the castle. It is a creepy place that looks as if it were carved right out of the mountain! You see a broken wooden door in the castle wall and decide to hide inside.

Looking back, you see a company of the Good Knight's soldiers fighting the orcs!

You dash through the doorway and enter a foul-smelling guardroom. In the dim light, you notice the rock glowing in your pocket.

"Thistle! Look at this rock I found in that dark tunnel. It's still glowing!"

"Let me see it," he says. You hand it to him, but the rock stops glowing! "It must work only for you, Molly," he says as he hands the stone back to you.

As the rock begins to glow again, you look at it very closely. Carved in the rock in tiny letters are the words "terra terro."

"Magical words!" you think to yourself as you put the stone back into your pocket.

At that moment, a wounded soldier stumbles into the room and falls down. You run to him and help him to sit up.

"Who are you?" he asks.

"I'm Molly and he's Thistle. We're trying to find his brother and my friend, who may be prisoners here."

"Prisoners are kept in the tower. But you must leave. Halfling! Take this young lass away from this evil place!" he orders.

"I can't! I must rescue my brother!" cries Thistle as he runs back out the door.

"Thistle, wait for me!" you call after him. You peek out the door, but he's gone.

Suddenly, you hear ferocious growling and see six ugly, yellow-skinned ogres come running out of the forest. With giant wooden clubs, they attack the soldiers.

Soon the Good Knight appears from behind the castle. With one swing of his sword, two of the huge monsters fall.

Another ogre knocks down two soldiers with its club and then looks at you!

If you want to run for the woods, turn to page 63.

If you want to pull the magic stone from your pocket, turn to page 67.

You and Thistle run down the mountain
and hide behind a clump of bushes. When
you peek back up the mountain, you see the
orcs fighting soldiers.

"I'm going home, Thistle," you tell him.
"I'd rather not be some monster's dinner!"

"Are you sure you can find your way back
alone?" he asks you sadly.

"I think so," you say. "I hope you find
your brother. Good-bye, Thistle."

"Good-bye, Molly," he says as he gives
you a hug. He turns and climbs back up the
mountain, staying away from the battle.

Now you're on your own. You climb down
the mountain until you reach a ledge. From
here, there is no safe way down.

A black bird flies up from the bushes
below you. Looking down, you see the ugly
green head of a troll! The huge monster
grins at you and grinds its teeth. It must be
very hungry!

The troll starts to climb up toward you.
You cry for help. Then, with a fluttering of
wings, a white flying horse lands on the
ledge beside you.

"Oh, a pegasus!" you exclaim as the winged horse bows. "Maybe you can help ."

Then you remember the two lumps of sugar in your pocket. You put one on the palm of your hand and say, "Here, Mr. Pegasus."

The flying horse moves toward you and nibbles the sugar hungrily from your hand.

Below you, the troll is getting closer and closer. "I'm afraid that nasty troll down there wants to catch me," you say.

"I'll give you some more sugar if you'll fly me away from here," you tell the horse. You stroke its mane. The horse nods its head. You climb onto its back, and it jumps into the air!

"Good-bye, hungry troll!" you shout.

Up and away you fly above the troll, the forest, and the mountain. The pegasus turns its head toward you for direction.

"I just want to go home," you say.

THE END

You dash to the golden doors, pull them open slightly, and squeeze through. The Good Knight and his men are fighting monsters around the throne. "This must be the throne room," you whisper to Thistle.

You duck behind a bubbling fountain and peek out. "Look! There's a skeleton wizard on the throne!" you tell Thistle.

"That must be Nightshade!" Thistle says.

Swords flash in the air, and two ogres fall. Seeing this, Nightshade shouts, "DIE BY FIRE!" A giant fire monster appears in the air above the throne! It blows a jet of fire, and the walls burst into flame!

Clutching your basket tightly, you feel something hard—the silver bowl!

"Let's get out of here before we're roasted!" says the frightened halfling.

If you want to use your silver bowl to throw water from the fountain onto the fire, turn to page 72.

If you want to run out of the fiery room, turn to page 75.

You grab Thistle's arm and pull him toward the stairs. "We'll hide down here. Come on!" you shout.

When you reach the bottom of the stairs, you hear a squeal. Looking back up the stairs, you see that a soldier is fighting the pig-faced orc guard.

Quickly, you step through the doorway into a dark cavern. To your left, a large fountain is bubbling in the corner. In the center of the huge cavern, you see a dozen soldiers fighting a red dragon.

The dragon rears up, and from its mouth comes a blaze of fire! The soldiers' clothing bursts into flames. They all start running around screaming.

Thinking fast, you pull the silver bowl out of your basket and fill it with water at the fountain. The bowl begins to glow!

Like smoke billowing up from a fire, a magical water creature streams up out of the bowl. It hangs in the air above you!

"It's a water elemental!" cries Thistle. "It will do whatever you tell it to do."

"Put out the fire!" you command it.
The elemental sprays the whole room.
The dragon is very angry. It lashes its
tail and blows a fireball at the elemental.

SSSSSss! The magic creature destroys
the fireball with a gush of water. Then it
sends a magic wave of water at the dragon.

The dragon and the elemental fade away!
But where the dragon stood, a bearded old
man in a red cloak appears.

"My, my," says the old man. "It's good to
be a wizard again! Nightshade turned me
into an evil red dragon five years ago."

"A wizard!" you exclaim. "Can you find
Thistle's brother and my friend?"

"Oh, I can do better than that!" says the
old wizard. He pulls a crystal ball from his
cloak, says a few magical words, and
POOF! The halfling and Garth appear!

"Hooray! It's my brother, Burr!" cheers
Thistle. The wizard smiles, says a few
words, and POOF! You're all sitting in the
moonberry patch on the hillside.

THE END

Choosing to leave the tower, you all run down the three flights of stairs and out the door at the bottom.

"Look!" you shout. "The Good Knight's soldiers are still fighting orcs in the courtyard and on the castle walls."

You all run toward the front gate, which remains unguarded. "Hurry!" cries Thistle as he heads down the road.

You make your way down the mountain and finally arrive back at your moonberry patch. The halflings show you and Garth their home, hidden on the hillside.

"You are both welcome to come and visit us anytime!" they tell you.

You and Garth leave your new friends and each head home. When you get home, your parents ask, "Where have you been?"

You tell them the whole story, but they don't believe you. Then someone knocks at the door. Garth and his parents come in.

Garth tells the story of where he spent the night and how YOU rescued him!

All eyes turn to you, the HERO!

THE END

Having made up your mind, you carefully unlock the door. The others run down the stairs in case something awful comes out.

You slowly pull the door open and look inside. A ghostly old man stands in the corner of the cell watching you. Behind him is a chair. You can see it right through him. He's a spectre!

"Hello," you say to the wispy man. "I've come to let you out!"

As the spectre floats slowly toward you, an evil grin appears on his face.

"Maybe this isn't such a good idea," you say to yourself. Quickly, you turn to leave, but it's too late!

As the spectre touches you, an icy chill goes up your spine. You start to feel strange and sick. You look at your hands and can see right through them!

You are now a spectre, too!

The old spectre laughs and flies out the door and down the stairs.

You have no choice but to follow . . . .

THE END

As the ogre approaches, you make a run for the woods. The ground shakes as the big monster turns and comes after you.

"Help!" you scream. When you reach the woods, an elf steps out of the trees and draws a long bow.

"Run, little one!" he shouts, aiming an arrow at the ogre. You stop behind a tree and watch. The brave elf shoots. TWANG!

The arrow hits its target, and the ogre falls into the brush with a loud crash.

"Good shot!" you cheer.

"Quickarrow the elf never misses!" he boasts to you with a wink.

You tell him your story and ask for directions home. He points out a path for you to follow and says, "I would take you home myself, but I must join the Good Knight."

"Good luck! And thanks," you say.

"Oh, and watch out for the umber hulk," he warns.

"The what?" you ask.

"It's a big creature with an insectlike head. If you look into its eyes, it will make you dizzy and confused."

"I'll watch out," you tell him. "Good-bye!"
You head off down the path.

Deep in the woods, you see that a large
tree has fallen across the path. Making
your way around the tree, you hear a twig
snap behind you.

You turn to look back and make out a
large dark shape through the trees.
Something is following you!

You look for some way to defend yourself
and remember the magic stone.

You reach into your pocket and pull it

out. The stone is still glowing. Then the ugliest creature you've ever seen pops its head through the trees behind you! It's the umber hulk!

You hold the stone above your head and shout the magic words, "TERRA TERRO!

"Take that, creature of evil!" you scream as you hurl the stone at its insectlike head.

The ground rumbles beneath your feet. Giant hands of rock and clay burst up out of the forest floor. You leap out of the way.

Tree-sized arms grab the umber hulk from below. The umber hulk stares into your eyes as it's dragged underground with the stone!

You become dizzy and confused! You wander out of the woods and somehow find your way home. When you get home, you can't remember what happened—only that something helped you. You're sure glad it did!

THE END

You pull the magic stone from your pocket and hold it up above your head. You sure hope this works! As the ogre moves closer you shout, "TERRA TERRO!"

Suddenly, the earth begins to shake. The ogre stops and looks around. Rocks fly up from the hillside as a giant rock man pulls himself up out of the ground!

When he stands up, he is as tall as the castle wall. Then he looks down at you.

"Help those good soldiers get rid of all the orcs and ogres!" you tell him.

The giant rock man nods and moves quickly toward the castle. He picks up an ogre and tosses it over the cliff.

Then he punches a big hole in the castle wall and grabs a handful of orcs. He flings them high over the trees into the woods.

The soldiers cheer! One by one the orcs and ogres are destroyed. Finally, there are no enemies in sight. The rock man winks at you and sinks back into the ground.

"Thank you, mighty rock man!" you say to the creature as it disappears slowly into the earth.

As you put the magic stone into your pocket, the soldiers lift you up onto their shoulders. "Hooray for the brave little girl!" they all shout.

The Good Knight walks over to you and asks, "What is your name?"

"I'm Molly," you tell him.

"You have helped to defeat the forces of evil in a wonderful way," he tells you with a smile. "Thank you. Now, tell me why you're here in such a dangerous place."

You tell him your story. Then he says, "Don't worry. We'll find your friends."

He turns to one of his soldiers and says, "Captain, see that this brave young lady is escorted home."

"Yes, sir!" The captain salutes.

"Good-bye, Lady Molly!" the Good Knight says and bows. "I must continue my battle against the evil Nightshade."

"Good-bye," you say. "And thank you."

The captain smiles at you, and you head for home.

THE END

You pull the bowl from your basket and dip it into the cold water of the fountain. As it fills with water, the bowl begins to glow, and something magical takes place.

"Thistle, look!" you whisper.

A stream of water comes shooting out of the bowl and hangs in the air above you. A water creature begins to take shape. It looks down at you.

"Put out the fire!" you command it.

With one breath, it sprays the room with water. All eyes turn to watch it attack the

fire monster. The monster hurls a fireball at the water creature. SSSsss! The fireball is destroyed by a wave of water.

Then a battle between fire and water begins. As the Good Knight runs to attack Nightshade, flame and spray turn the room into a steam bath. The two monsters destroy each other in a terrible fight. The silver bowl shatters!

Nightshade stands up and waves his skeleton fingers in the air. "LIGHT INTO NIGHT!" he cries. Everything turns black.

You can't see a thing. Then you look down and notice that your moonberries are beginning to glow! That must be why they're called MOONberries—they glow in the dark.

"Find Nightshade!" the Good Knight shouts. "Don't let him escape!"

You stand up and fling your basket of berries in the direction of the throne. The glowing berries spill out all over the floor. You can just make out Nightshade opening a secret door behind the throne.

The Good Knight can see Nightshade,

too. He runs to the throne, swings his sword, and destroys the evil skeleton at last!

Suddenly, the castle begins to crumble into dust. The monsters disappear.

You run outside and see the tower door fly open. Out runs a halfling followed by your friend Garth!

"It's my brother, Burr!" cries Thistle.

"We found them!" you say. "Our quest is done. Let's go home!"

THE END

"Wait until the fire monster looks away. Then run for the door!" you tell Thistle.

"Evil has no hope!" shouts Sir Gregor. You turn around and see the Good Knight throw his magical sword at the fire monster. The silver sword glows as it strikes the monster's flaming body. The monster howls in pain and fills the room with fire!

You rush out the doorway with soldiers following close behind you. The Good Knight recovers his sword, runs through the doors, and slams them shut behind him.

KABOOM! A loud explosion blows the roof off the palace! The dark image of a skull appears in the clouds of smoke above. It is the face of Nightshade! As it fades, you hear, "NIGHTSHADE WILL RETURN!"

The ground shakes, and the castle begins to crumble. All the monsters vanish!

The tower door flies open, and you see your friend Garth running toward you followed by a halfling. "It's my brother, Burr!" cries Thistle.

"Hooray!" you shout. "We found them!"

THE END

FANTASY FOREST™ Books

Is your dragon dragging?

Do you both need to go on an adventure?

Why not Pick a Path to Adventure™ with these FANTASY FOREST™ Books?

#1 THE RING, THE SWORD, AND THE UNICORN
#2 RUINS OF RANGAR
#3 SHADOWCASTLE
#4 KEEP OF THE ANCIENT KING

From the producers of the DUNGEONS & DRAGONS® Game

ENDLESS QUEST™ Books

From the producers of the DUNGEONS & DRAGONS® Game

#1 DUNGEON OF DREAD

#2 MOUNTAIN OF MIRRORS

#3 PILLARS OF PENTEGARN

#4 RETURN TO BROOKMERE

#5 REVOLT OF THE DWARVES

#6 REVENGE OF THE RAINBOW DRAGONS

#7 HERO OF WASHINGTON SQUARE
based on the TOP SECRET™ Game

#8 VILLAINS OF VOLTURNUS
based on the STAR FRONTIERS™ Game

#9 ROBBERS AND ROBOTS
based on the TOP SECRET™ Game

#10 CIRCUS OF FEAR

#11 SPELL OF THE WINTER WIZARD

#12 LIGHT ON QUESTS MOUNTAIN
based on the GAMMA WORLD™ Game

For a free catalog, write:
TSR Hobbies, Inc.
P.O. Box 756, Dept. EQB
Lake Geneva, WI 53147

TSR Hobbies, Inc.